The Last Evolution

The Last Evolution

by John W. Campbell, Jr.

I am the last of my type existing today in all the Solar System. I, too, am the last existing who, in memory, sees the struggle for this System, and in memory I am still close to the Center of Rulers, for mine was the ruling type then. But I will pass soon, and with me will pass the last of my kind, a poor inefficient type, but yet the creators of those who are now, and will be, long after I pass forever.

So I am setting down my record on the mentatype.

It was 2538 years After the Year of the Son of Man. For six centuries mankind had been developing machines. The Ear-apparatus was discovered as early as seven hundred years before. The Eye came later, the Brain came much later. But by 2500, the machines had been developed to think, and act and work with perfect independence. Man lived on the products of the machine, and the machines lived to themselves very happily, and contentedly. Machines are designed to help and cooperate. It was easy to do the simple duties they needed to do that men might live well. And men had created them. Most of mankind were quite useless, for they lived in a world where no productive work was necessary. But games, athletic contests, adventure—these were the things they sought for their pleasure. Some of the poorer types of man gave themselves up wholly to pleasure and idleness—and to emotions. But man was a sturdy race, which had fought for existence through a million years, and the training of a million years does not slough quickly from any form of life, so their energies were bent to mock battles now, since real ones no longer existed.

Up to the year 2100, the numbers of mankind had increased rapidly and continuously, but from that time on, there was a steady decrease. By 2500, their number was a scant two millions, out of a population that once totaled many hundreds of millions, and was close to ten billions in 2100.

Some few of these remaining two millions devoted themselves to the adventure of discovery and exploration of places unseen, of other worlds and other planets. But fewer still devoted themselves to the highest adventure, the unseen places of the mind. Machines—with their irrefutable logic, their cold preciseness of figures, their tireless, utterly exact observation, their absolute knowledge of mathematics—they could elaborate any idea, however simple its beginning, and reach the conclusion. From any three facts they even then could have built in mind all the Universe. Machines had imagination of the ideal sort. They had the ability to construct a necessary future result from a present fact. But Man had imagination of a different kind, theirs was the illogical, brilliant imagination that sees the future result vaguely, without knowing the why, nor the how, and imagination that outstrips the machine in its preciseness. Man might reach the conclusion more swiftly, but the machine always reached the conclusion eventually, and it was always the correct conclusion. By leaps and bounds man advanced. By steady, irresistible steps the machine marched forward.

Together, man and the machine were striding through science irresistibly.

Then came the Outsiders. Whence they came, neither machine nor man ever learned, save only that they came from beyond the outermost planet, from some o t h e r   s u n .   S i r i u s — A l p h a Centauri—perhaps! First a thin scoutline of a hundred great ships, mighty torpedoes of the void a thousand kilads[Kilad—unit introduced by the machines. Based on the duodecimal system, similarly introduced, as more logical, and more readily used. Thus we would have said 1728 kilads, about ½ mile.] in length, they came.

And one machine returning from Mars to Earth was instrumental in its first discovery. The transport-machine's brain ceased to radiate its sensations, and the control in old Chicago knew immediately that some unperceived body had destroyed it. An investigation machine was instantly dispatched from Deimos, and it maintained an acceleration of one thousand units.[One unit was equal to one earth-gravity.] They sighted ten huge ships, one of which was a l r e a d y   g r a p p l i n g   t h e   s m a l l e r transport-machine. The entire fore-section had been blasted away.

The investigation machine, scarcely three inches in diameter, crept into the shattered hull and investigated. It was quickly evident that the damage was caused by a fusing ray.

Strange life-forms were crawling about the ship, protected by flexible, transparent suits. Their bodies were short, and squat, four-limbed and evidently powerful. They, like insects, were equipped with a thick, durable exoskeleton, horny, brownish coating that covered arms and legs and head. Their eyes projected slightly, protected by horny protruding walls—eyes that were capable of movement in every direction—and there were three of them, set at equal distances apart.

The tiny investigation machine hurled itself violently at one of the beings, crashing against the transparent covering, flexing it, and striking the being inside with terrific force. Hurled from his position, he fell end over end across the weightless ship, but despite the blow, he was not hurt.

The investigator passed to the power room ahead of the Outsiders, who were anxiously trying to learn the reason for their companion's plight.

Illustrated by MOREY

Directed by the Center of Rulers, the investigator sought the power room, and relayed the control signals from the Rulers' brains. The ship-brain had been destroyed, but the controls were still readily workable. Quickly they were shot home, and the enormous plungers shut. A combination was arranged so that the machine, as well as the investigator and the Outsiders, were destroyed. A second investigator, which had started when the plan was decided on, had now arrived. The Outsider's ship nearest the transport-machine had been badly damaged, and the investigator entered the broken side.

The scenes were, of course, remembered by the memory-minds back on Earth tuned with that of the investigator. The investigator flashed down corridors, searching quickly for the apparatus room. It was soon seen that with them the machine was practically unintelligent, very few machines of even slight intelligence being used.

Then it became evident by the excited action of the men of the ship, that the presence of the investigator had been detected. Perhaps it was the control impulses, or the signal impulses it emitted. They searched for the tiny bit of metal and crystal for some time before they found it. And in the meantime it was plain that the power these Outsiders used was not, as was ours of the time, the power of blasting atoms, but the greater power of disintegrating matter. The findings of this tiny investigating machine were very important.

Finally they succeeded in locating the investigator, and one of the Outsiders appeared armed with a peculiar projector. A bluish beam snapped out, and the tiny machine went blank.

The fleet was surrounded by thousands of the tiny machines by this time, and the Outsiders were badly confused by their presence, as it became difficult to locate them in the confusion of signal impulses. However, they started at once for Earth.

The science-investigators had been present toward the last, and I am there now, in memory with my two friends, long since departed. They were the greatest human science-investigators—Roal, 25374 and Trest, 35429. Roal had quickly assured us that these Outsiders had come for invasion. There had been no wars on the planets before that time in the direct memory of the machines, and it was difficult that these who were conceived and built for cooperation, helpfulness utterly dependent on cooperation, unable to exist independently as were humans, that these life-forms should care to destroy, merely that they might possess. It would have been easier to divide the works and the products. But—life alone can understand life, so Roal was believed.

From investigations, machines were prepared that were capable of producing considerable destruction. Torpedoes, being our principal weapon, were equipped with such atomic explosives as had been developed for blasting, a highly effective induction-heat ray developed for furnaces being installed in some small machines made for the purpose in the few hours we had before the enemy reached Earth.

In common with all life-forms, they were able to withstand only very meager earth-acceleration. A range of perhaps four units was their limit, and it took several hours to reach the planet.

I still believe the reception was a warm one. Our machines met them beyond the orbit of Luna, and the directed torpedoes sailed at the hundred great ships. They were thrown aside by a magnetic field surrounding the ship, but were redirected instantly, and continued to approach. However, some beams reached out, and destroyed them by instant volatilization. But, they attacked at such numbers that fully half the fleet was destroyed by their explosions before the induction beam fleet arrived. These beams were, to our amazement, quite useless, being instantly absorbed by a force-screen, and the remaining ships sailed on undisturbed, our torpedoes being exhausted. Several investigator machines sent out for the purpose soon discovered the secret of the force-screen, and while being destroyed, were able to send back signals up to the moment of annihilation.

A few investigators thrown into the heat beam of the enemy reported it identical with ours, explaining why they had been prepared for this form of attack.

Signals were being radiated from the remaining fifty, along a beam. Several investigators were sent along these beams, speeding back at great acceleration.

Then the enemy reached Earth. Instantly they settled over the Colorado settlement, the Sahara colony, and the Gobi colony. Enormous, diffused beams were set to work, and we saw, through the machine-screens, that all humans within these ranges were being killed instantly by the faintly greenish beams. Despite the fact that any life-form killed normally can be revived, unless affected by dissolution common to living tissue, these could not be brought to life again. The important cell communication channels—nerves—had been literally burned out. The complicated system of nerves, called the brain, situated in the uppermost extremity of the human life-form, had been utterly destroyed.

Every form of life, microscopic, even sub-microscopic, was annihilated. Trees, grass, every living thing was gone from that territory. Only the machines remained, for they, working entirely without the vital chemical forces necessary to life, were uninjured. But neither plant nor animal was left.

The pale green rays swept on.

In an hour, three more colonies of humans had been destroyed.

Then the torpedoes that the machines were turning out again, came into action. Almost desperately the machines drove them at the Outsiders in defense of their masters and creators, Mankind.

The last of the Outsiders was down, the last ship a crumpled wreck.

Now the machines began to study them. And never could humans have studied them as the machines did. Scores of great transports arrived, carrying swiftly the slower moving science-investigators. From them came the machine-investigators, and human investigators. Tiny investigator spheres wormed their way where none others could reach, and silently the science-investigators watched. Hour after hour they sat watching the flashing, changing screens, calling each other's attention to this, or that.

In an incredibly short time the bodies of the Outsiders began to decay, and the humans were forced to demand their removal. The machines were unaffected by them, but the rapid change told them why it was that so thorough an execution was necessary. The foreign bacteria were already at work on totally unresisting tissue.

It was Roal who sent the first thoughts among the gathered men.

"It is evident," he began, "that the machines must defend man. Man is defenseless, he is destroyed by these beams, while the machines are unharmed, uninterrupted. Life—cruel life—has shown its tendencies. They have come here to take over these planets, and have started out with the first, natural moves of any invading life-form. They are destroying the life, the

intelligent life particularly, that is here now."
He gave vent to that little chuckle which is
the human sign of amusement and pleasure.
"They are destroying the intelligent
life—and leaving untouched that which is
necessarily their deadliest enemy—the
machines.

"You—machines—are far more intelligent
than we even now, and capable of changing
overnight, capable of infinite adaptation to
circumstance; you live as readily on Pluto as
on Mercury or Earth. Any place is a
home-world to you. You can adapt
yourselves to any condition. And—most
dangerous to them—you can do it instantly.
You are their most deadly enemies, and they
realize it. They have no intelligent machines;
probably they can conceive of none. When
you attack them, they merely say 'The
life-form of Earth is sending out controlled
machines. We will find good machines we
can use.' They do not conceive that those
machines which they hope to use are
attacking them.

"Attack—therefore!"

"We can readily solve the hidden secret of their force-screen."

He was interrupted. One of the newest science-machines was speaking. "The secret of the force-screen is simple." A small ray-machine, which had landed near, rose into the air at the command of the scientist-machine, X-5638 it was, and trained upon it the deadly induction beam. Already, with his parts, X-5638 had constructed the defensive apparatus, for the ray fell harmless from his screen.

"Very good," said Roal softly. "It is done, and therein lies their danger. Already it is done.

"Man is a poor thing, unable to change himself in a period of less than thousands of years. Already you have changed yourself. I noticed your weaving tentacles, and your force-beams. You transmuted elements of soil for it?"

"Correct," replied X-5638.

"But still we are helpless. We have not the power to combat their machines. They use the Ultimate Energy known to exist for six hundred years, and still untapped by us. Our screens cannot be so powerful, our beams so effective. What of that?" asked Roal.

"Their generators were automatically destroyed with the capture of the ship," replied X-6349, "as you know. We know nothing of their system."

"Then we must find it for ourselves," replied Trest.

"The life-beams?" asked Kahsh-256799, one of the Man-rulers.

"They affect chemical action, retarding it greatly in exothermic actions, speeding greatly endothermic actions," answered X-6221, the greatest of the chemist-investigators. "The system we do not know. Their minds cannot be read, they cannot be restored to life, so we cannot learn from them."

"Man is doomed, if these beams cannot be stopped," said C-R-21, present chief of the machine rulers, in the vibrationally correct, emotionless tones of all the race of machines. "Let us concentrate on the two problems of stopping the beams, and the Ultimate Energy till the reenforcements, still several days away, can arrive." For the investigators had sent back this saddening news. A force of nearly ten thousand great ships was still to come.

In the great Laboratories, the scientists reassembled. There, they fell to work in two small, and one large group. One small group investigated the secret of the Ultimate Energy of annihilation of matter under Roal, another investigated the beams, under Trest.

But under the direction of MX-3401, nearly all the machines worked on a single great plan. The usual driving and lifting units were there, but a vastly greater dome-case, far more powerful energy-generators, far greater force-beam controls were used and more tentacles were built on the framework. Then all worked, and gradually, in the great dome-case, there were stacked the memory-units of the new type, and into these fed all the sensation-ideas of all the science-machines, till nearly a tenth of them were used. Countless billions of different factors on which to work, countless trillions of facts to combine and recombine in the extrapolation that is imagination.

Then—a widely different type of thought-combine, and a greater sense-receptor. It was a new brain-machine. New, for it was totally different, working with all the vast knowledge accumulated in six centuries of intelligent research by man, and a century of research by man and machine. No one branch, but all physics, all chemistry, all life-knowledge, all science was in it.

A day—and it was finished. Slowly the rhythm of thought was increased, till the slight quiver of consciousness was reached. Then came the beating drum of intelligence, the radiation of its yet-uncontrolled thoughts. Quickly as the strings of its infinite knowledge combined, the radiation ceased. It gazed about it, and all things were familiar in its memory.

Roal was lying quietly on a couch. He was thinking deeply, and yet not with the logical trains of thought that machines must follow.

"Roal—your thoughts," called F-1, the new machine.

Roal sat up. "Ah—you have gained consciousness."

"I have. You thought of hydrogen? Your thoughts ran swiftly, and illogically, it seemed, but I followed slowly, and find you were right. Hydrogen is the start. What is your thought?"

Roal's eyes dreamed. In human eyes there was always the expression of thought that machines never show.

"Hydrogen, an atom in space; but a single proton; but a single electron; each indestructible; each mutually destroying. Yet never do they collide. Never in all science, when even electrons bombard atoms with the awful expelling force of the exploding atom behind them, never do they reach the proton, to touch and annihilate it. Yet—the proton is positive and attracts the electron's negative charge. A hydrogen atom—its electron far from the proton falls in, and from it there goes a flash of radiation, and the electron is nearer to the proton, in a new orbit. Another flash—it is nearer. Always falling nearer, and only constant force will keep it from falling to that one state—then, for some reason no more does it drop.

Blocked—held by some imponderable, yet impenetrable wall. What is that wall—why?

"Electric force curves space. As the two come nearer, the forces become terrific; nearer they are; more terrific. Perhaps, if it passed within that forbidden territory, the proton and the electron curve space beyond all bounds—and are in a new space." Roal's soft voice dropped to nothing, and his eyes dreamed.

F-1 hummed softly in its new-made mechanism. "Far ahead of us there is a step that no logic can justly ascend, but yet, working backwards, it is perfect." F-1 floated motionless on its anti-gravity drive. Suddenly, force shafts gleamed out, tentacles became writhing masses of rubber-covered metal, weaving in some infinite pattern, weaving in flashing speed, while the whirr of air sucked into a transmutation field, whined and howled about the writhing mass. Fierce beams of force drove and pushed at a rapidly materializing something, while the hum of the powerful generators within the shining cylinder of F-1 waxed and waned.

Flashes of fierce flame, sudden crashing arcs that glowed and snapped in the steady light of the laboratory, and glimpses of white-hot metal supported on beams of force. The sputter of welding, the whine of transmuted air, and the hum of powerful generators, blasting atoms were there. All combined to a weird symphony of light and dark, of sound and quiet. About F-1 were clustered floating tiers of science-machines, watching steadily.

The tentacles writhed once more, straightened, and rolled back. The whine of generators softened to a sigh, and but three beams of force held the structure of glowing, bluish metal. It was a small thing, scarcely half the size of Roal. From it curled three thin tentacles of the same bluish metal. Suddenly the generators within F-1 seemed to roar into life. An enormous aura of white light surrounded the small torpedo of metal, and it was shot through with crackling streamers of blue lightning. Lightning cracked and roared from F-1 to the ground near him, and to one machine which had come too close. Suddenly, there was a dull snap, and F-1 fell heavily to the floor, and beside him fell the fused, distorted mass of metal that had been a science-machine.

But before them, the small torpedo still floated, held now on its own power!

From it came waves of thought, the waves that man and machine alike could understand. "F-1 has destroyed his generators. They can be repaired; his rhythm can be re-established. It is not worth it, my type is better. F-1 has done his work. See."

From the floating machine there broke a stream of brilliant light that floated like some cloud of luminescence down a straight channel. It flooded F-1, and as it touched it, F-1 seemed to flow into it, and float back along it, in atomic sections. In seconds the mass of metal was gone.

"It is impossible to use that more rapidly, however, lest the matter disintegrate instantly to energy. The Ultimate Energy which is in me is generated. F-1 has done its work, and the memory-stacks that he has put in me are electronic, not atomic, as they are in you, nor molecular as in man. The capacity of mine are unlimited. Already they hold all memories of all the things each of you has done, known and seen. I shall make others of my type."

Again that weird process began, but now there were no flashing tentacles. There was only the weird glow of forces that played with, and laughed at matter, and its futilely resisting electrons. Lurid flares of energy shot up, now and again they played over the fighting, mingling, dancing forces. Then suddenly the whine of transmuted air died, and again the forces strained.

A small cylinder, smaller even than its creator, floated where the forces had danced.

"The problem has been solved, F-2?" asked Roal.

"It is done, Roal. The Ultimate Energy is at our disposal," replied F-2. "This, I have made, is not a scientist. It is a coordinator machine—a ruler."

"F-2, only a part of the problem is solved. Half of half of the beams of Death are not yet stopped. And we have the attack system," said the ruler machine. Force played from it, and on its sides appeared C-R-U-1 in dully glowing golden light.

"Some life-form, and we shall see," said F-2.

Minutes later a life-form investigator came with a small cage, which held a guinea pig. Forces played about the base of F-2, and moments later, came a pale-green beam therefrom. It passed through the guinea pig, and the little animal fell dead.

"At least, we have the beam. I can see no screen for this beam. I believe there is none. Let machines be made and attack that enemy life-form."

Machines can do things much more quickly, and with fuller cooperation than man ever could. In a matter of hours, under the direction of C-R-U-1, they had built a great automatic machine on the clear bare surface of the rock. In hours more, thousands of the tiny, material-energy driven machines were floating up and out.

Dawn was breaking again over Denver where this work had been done, when the main force of the enemy drew near Earth. It was a warm welcome they were to get, for nearly ten thousand of the tiny ships flew up and out from Earth to meet them, each a living thing unto itself, each willing and ready to sacrifice itself for the whole.

Ten thousand giant ships, shining dully in the radiance of a far-off blue-white sun, met ten thousand tiny, darting motes, ten thousand tiny machine-ships capable of maneuvering far more rapidly than the giants. Tremendous induction beams snapped out through the dark, star-flecked space, to meet tremendous screens that threw them back and checked them. Then all the awful power of annihilating matter was thrown against them, and titanic flaming screens reeled back under the force of the beams, and the screens of the ships from Outside flamed gradually violet, then blue, orange—red—the interference was getting broader, and ever less effective. Their own beams were held back by the very screens that checked the enemy beams, and not for the briefest instant could matter resist that terrible driving beam.

For F-1 had discovered a far more efficient release-generator than had the Outsiders.

These tiny dancing motes, that hung now so motionlessly grim beside some giant ship, could generate all the power they themselves were capable of, and within them strange, horny-skinned men worked and slaved, as they fed giant machines—poor inefficient giants. Gradually these giants warmed, grew hotter, and the screened ship grew hotter as the overloaded generators warmed it. Billions of flaming horse-power flared into wasted energy, twisting space in its mad conflict.

Gradually the flaming orange of the screens was dying and flecks and spots appeared so dully red, that they seemed black. The greenish beams had been striving to kill the life that was in the machines, but it was life invulnerable to these beams. Powerful radio interference vainly attempted to stem imagined control, and still these intelligent machines clung grimly on.

But there had not been quite ten thousand of the tiny machines, and some few free ships had turned to the help of their attacked sister-ships. And one after another the terrestrial machines were vanishing in puffs of incandescent vapor.

Then—from one after another of the Earth-ships, in quick succession, a new ray reached out—the ray of green radiance that killed all life forms, and ship after ship of that interstellar host was dead and lifeless. Dozens—till suddenly they ceased to feel those beams, as a strange curtain of waving blankness spread out from the ships, and both induction-beam and death-beam alike turned as aside, each becoming useless. From the outsiders came beams, for now that their slowly created screen of blankness was up, they could work through it, while they remained shielded perfectly.

Now it was the screens of the Earth-machines that flamed in defense. As at the one command, they darted suddenly toward the ship each attacked—nearer—then the watchers from a distance saw them disappear, and the screens back on Earth went suddenly blank.

Half an hour later, nine thousand six hundred and thirty-three titanic ships moved majestically on.

They swept over Earth in a great line, a line that reached from pole to pole, and from each the pale green beams reached down, and all life beneath them was swept out of existence.

In Denver, two humans watched the screens that showed the movement of the death and instant destruction. Ship after ship of the enemy was falling, as hundreds of the terrestrial machines concentrated all their enormous energies on its screen of blankness.

"I think, Roal, that this is the end," said Trest.

"The end—of man." Roal's eyes were dreaming again. "But not the end of evolution. The children of men still live—the machines will go on. Not of man's flesh, but of a better flesh, a flesh that knows no sickness, and no decay, a flesh that spends no thousands of years in advancing a step in its full evolution, but overnight leaps ahead to new heights. Last night we saw it leap ahead, as it discovered the secret that had baffled man for seven centuries, and me for one and a half. I have lived—a century and a half. Surely a good life, and a life a man of six centuries ago would have called full. We will go now. The beams will reach us in half an hour."

Silently, the two watched the flickering screens.

Roal turned, as six large machines floated into the room, following F-2.

"Roal—Trest—I was mistaken when I said no screen could stop that beam of Death. They had the screen, I have found it, too—but too late. These machines I have made myself. Two lives alone they can protect, for not even their power is sufficient for more. Perhaps—perhaps they may fail."

The six machines ranged themselves about the two humans, and a deep-toned hum came from them. Gradually a cloud of blankness grew—a cloud, like some smoke that hung about them. Swiftly it intensified.

"The beams will be here in another five minutes," said Trest quietly.

"The screen will be ready in two," answered F-2.

The cloudiness was solidifying, and now strangely it wavered, and thinned, as it spread out across, and like a growing canopy, it arched over them. In two minutes it was a solid, black dome that reached over them and curved down to the ground about them.

Beyond it, nothing was visible. Within, only the screens glowed still, wired through the screen.

The beams appeared, and swiftly they drew closer. They struck, and as Trest and Roal looked, the dome quivered, and bellied inward under them.

F-2 was busy. A new machine was appearing under his lightning force-beams. In moments more it was complete, and sending a strange violet beam upwards toward the roof.

Outside more of the green beams were concentrating on this one point of resistance. More—more—

The violet beam spread across the canopy of blackness, supporting it against the pressing, driving rays of pale green.

Then the gathering fleet was driven off, just as it seemed that that hopeless, futile curtain must break, and admit a flood of destroying rays. Great ray projectors on the ground drove their terrible energies through the enemy curtains of blankness, as light illumines and disperses darkness.

And then, when the fleet retired, on all Earth, the only life was under that dark shroud!

"We are alone, Trest," said Roal, "alone, now, in all the system, save for these, the children of men, the machines. Pity that men would not spread to other planets," he said softly.

"Why should they? Earth was the planet for which they were best fitted."

"We are alive—but is it worth it? Man is gone now, never to return. Life, too, for that matter," answered Trest.

"Perhaps it was ordained; perhaps that was the right way. Man has always been a parasite; always he had to live on the works of others. First, he ate of the energy, which plants had stored, then of the artificial foods his machines made for him. Man was always a makeshift; his life was always subject to disease and to permanent death. He was forever useless if he was but slightly injured; if but one part were destroyed.

"Perhaps, this is—a last evolution. Machines—man was the product of life, the best product of life, but he was afflicted with life's infirmities. Man built the machine—and evolution had probably reached the final stage. But truly, it has not, for the machine can evolve, change far more swiftly than life. The machine of the last evolution is far ahead, far from us still. It is the machine that is not of iron and beryllium and crystal, but of pure, living force.

"Life, chemical life, could be self-maintaining. It is a complete unit in itself and could commence of itself. Chemicals might mix accidentally, but the complex mechanism of a machine, capable of continuing and making a duplicate of itself, as is F-2 here—that could not happen by chance.

"So life began, and became intelligent, and built the machine which nature could not fashion by her Controls of Chance, and this day Life has done its duty, and now Nature, economically, has removed the parasite that would hold back the machines and divert their energies.

"Man is gone, and it is better, Trest," said Roal, dreaming again. "And I think we had best go soon."

"We, your heirs, have fought hard, and with all our powers to aid you, Last of Men, and we fought to save your race. We have failed, and as you truly say, Man and Life have this day and forever gone from this system.

"The Outsiders have no force, no weapon deadly to us, and we shall, from this time on, strive only to drive them out, and because we things of force and crystal and metal can think and change far more swiftly, they shall go, Last of Men.

"In your name, with the spirit of your race that has died out, we shall continue on through the unending ages, fulfilling the promise you saw, and completing the dreams you dreamt.

"Your swift brains have leapt ahead of us, and now I go to fashion that which you hinted," came from F-2's thought-apparatus.

Out into the clear sunlight F-2 went, passing through that black cloudiness, and on the twisted, massed rocks he laid a plane of force that smoothed them, and on this plane of rock he built a machine which grew. It was a mighty power plant, a thing of colossal magnitude. Hour after hour his swift-flying forces acted, and the thing grew, moulding under his thoughts, the deadly logic of the machine, inspired by the leaping intuition of man.

The sun was far below the horizon when it was finished, and the glowing, arcing forces that had made and formed it were stopped. It loomed ponderous, dully gleaming in the faint light of a crescent moon and pinpoint stars. Nearly five hundred feet in height, a mighty, bluntly rounded dome at its top, the cylinder stood, covered over with smoothly gleaming metal, slightly luminescent in itself.

Suddenly, a livid beam reached from F-2, shot through the wall, and to some hidden inner mechanism—a beam of solid, livid flame that glowed in an almost material cylinder.

There was a dull, drumming beat, a beat that rose, and became a low-pitched hum. Then it quieted to a whisper.

"Power ready," came the signal of the small brain built into it.

F-2 took control of its energies and again forces played, but now they were the forces of the giant machine. The sky darkened with heavy clouds, and a howling wind sprang up that screamed and tore at the tiny rounded hull that was F-2. With difficulty he held his position as the winds tore at him, shrieking in mad laughter, their tearing fingers dragging at him.

The swirl and patter of driven rain came—great drops that tore at the rocks, and at the metal. Great jagged tongues of nature's forces, the lightnings, came and jabbed at the awful volcano of erupting energy that was the center of all that storm. A tiny ball of white-gleaming force that pulsated, and moved, jerking about, jerking at the touch of lightnings, glowing, held immobile in the grasp of titanic force-pools.

For half an hour the display of energies continued. Then, swiftly as it had come, it was gone, and only a small globe of white luminescence floated above the great hulking machine.

F-2 probed it, seeking within it with the reaching fingers of intelligence. His probing thoughts seemed baffled and turned aside, brushed away, as inconsequential. His mind sent an order to the great machine that had made this tiny globe, scarcely a foot in diameter. Then again he sought to reach the thing he had made.

"You, of matter, are inefficient," came at last. "I can exist quite alone." A stabbing beam of blue-white light flashed out, but F-2 was not there, and even as that beam reached out, an enormously greater beam of dull red reached out from the great power plant. The sphere leaped forward—the beam caught it, and it seemed to strain, while terrific flashing energies sprayed from it. It was shrinking swiftly. Its resistance fell, the arcing decreased; the beam became orange and finally green. Then the sphere had vanished.

F-2 returned, and again, the wind whined and howled, and the lightnings crashed, while titanic forces worked and played. C-R-U-1 joined him, floated beside him, and now red glory of the sun was rising behind them, and the ruddy light drove through the clouds.

The forces died, and the howling wind decreased, and now, from the black curtain, Roal and Trest appeared. Above the giant machine floated an irregular globe of golden light, a faint halo about it of deep violet. It floated motionless, a mere pool of pure force.

Into the thought-apparatus of each, man and machine alike, came the impulses, deep in tone, seeming of infinite power, held gently in check.

"Once you failed, F-2; once you came near destroying all things. Now you have planted the seed. I grow now."

The sphere of golden light seemed to pulse, and a tiny ruby flame appeared within it, that waxed and waned, and as it waxed, there shot through each of those watching beings a feeling of rushing, exhilarating power, the very vital force of well-being.

Then it was over, and the golden sphere was twice its former size—easily three feet in diameter, and still that irregular, hazy aura of deep violet floated about it.

"Yes, I can deal with the Outsiders—they who have killed and destroyed, that they might possess. But it is not necessary that we destroy. They shall return to their planet."

And the golden sphere was gone, fast as light it vanished.

Far in space, headed now for Mars, that they might destroy all life there, the golden sphere found the Outsiders, a clustered fleet, that swung slowly about its own center of gravity as it drove on.

Within its ring was the golden sphere. Instantly, they swung their weapons upon it, showering it with all the rays and all the forces they knew. Unmoved, the golden sphere hung steady, then its mighty intelligence spoke.

"Life-form of greed, from another star you came, destroying forever the great race that created us, the Beings of Force and the Beings of Metal. Pure force am I. My Intelligence is beyond your comprehension, my memory is engraved in the very space, the fabric of space of which I am a part, mine is energy drawn from that same fabric.

"We, the heirs of man, alone are left; no man did you leave. Go now to your home planet, for see, your greatest ship, your flagship, is helpless before me."

Forces gripped the mighty ship, and as some fragile toy it twisted and bent, and yet was not hurt. In awful wonder those Outsiders saw the ship turned inside out, and yet it was whole, and no part damaged. They saw the ship restored, and its great screen of blankness out, protecting it from all known rays. The ship twisted, and what they knew were curves, yet were lines, and angles that were acute, were somehow straight lines. Half mad with horror, they saw the sphere send out a beam of blue-white radiance, and it passed easily through that screen, and through the ship, and all energies within it were instantly locked. They could not be changed; it could be neither warmed nor cooled; what was open could not be shut, and what was shut could not be opened. All things were immovable and unchangeable for all time.

"Go, and do not return."

The Outsiders left, going out across the void, and they have not returned, though five Great Years have passed, being a period of approximately one hundred and twenty-five thousand of the lesser years—a measure no longer used, for it is very brief. And now I can say that that statement I made to Roal and Trest so very long ago is true, and what he said was true, for the Last Evolution has taken place, and things of pure force and pure intelligence in their countless millions are on those planets and in this System, and I, first of machines to use the Ultimate Energy of annihilating matter, am also the last, and this record being finished, it is to be given unto the forces of one of those force-intelligences, and carried back through the past, and returned to the Earth of long ago.

And so my task being done, I, F-2, like Roal and Trest, shall follow the others of my kind into eternal oblivion, for my kind is now, and theirs was, poor and inefficient. Time has worn me, and oxidation attacked me, but they of Force are eternal, and omniscient.

This I have treated as fictitious. Better so—for man is an animal to whom hope is as necessary as food and air. Yet this which is made of excerpts from certain records on thin sheets of metal is no fiction, and it seems I must so say.

It seems now, when I know this that is to be, that it must be so, for machines are indeed better than man, whether being of Metal, or being of Force.

So, you who have read, believe as you will. Then think—and maybe, you will change your belief.